nature's perfect package

egg

steve jenkins & robin page

HOUGHTON MIFFLIN HARCOURT   BOSTON   NEW YORK

Butterflies,
frogs, sharks, and
humans all begin life as
an egg. So does almost every
other animal. The eggs of some
creatures — including most mammals
— are nurtured inside their mother's
body, where they develop into babies
that are born alive. But many more animals
lay their eggs — either one at a time, by
the dozens, or by the millions. Eggs come
in a fantastic range of sizes, shapes,
and colors. Animals that lay eggs bury
them, carry them, guard them, or
simply leave them alone. And
each egg contains everything
needed to create a new
living creature.

Egg layers

Slugs, sea urchins, and most other simple animals lay eggs. All insects, spiders, amphibians, and birds are egg layers. A few fish and reptiles give birth to live babies, but most lay eggs. And two mammals — the echidna and platypus — also lay eggs.

banana slug   **sea urchin**   **potato beetle**   **tarantula**   **leopard frog**

Except for the crow egg, which is shown life-size, these eggs are greatly enlarged.

Silhouettes at the bottom of the page show the actual size of the eggs.

scorpion fish

skink

crow

echidna

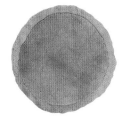

Little eggs, big eggs

Some eggs are too small to see without a microscope. Others — including some laid by animals that are extinct — are enormous. The eggs on the next four pages are shown at actual size.

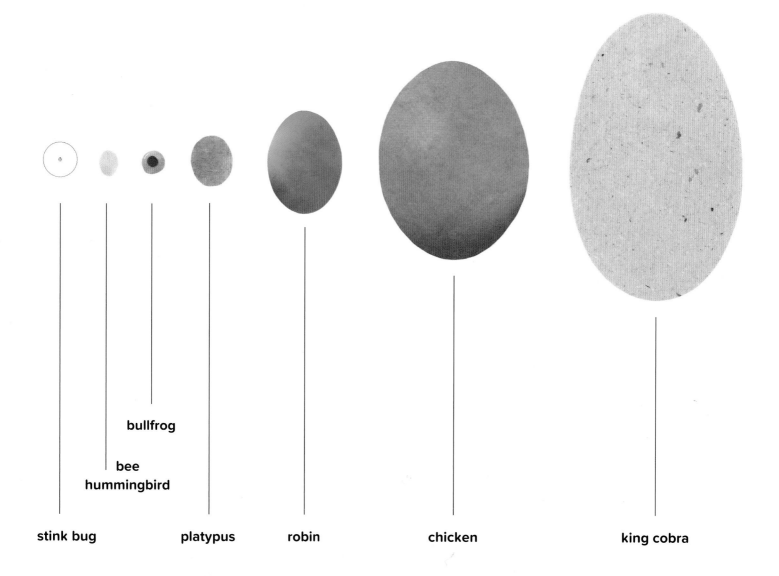

bullfrog

bee
hummingbird

stink bug   platypus   robin   chicken   king cobra

ostrich
(the largest egg of any
living creature)

elephant bird
(hunted to extinction in
the 1700s)

elephant bird

kiwi

chicken

giant
squid

gigantoraptor
(the fossilized egg of a dinosaur that
lived about 80 million years ago)

Sometimes big animals lay big eggs, but not always. The egg of the kiwi, a bird smaller than a chicken, is thousands of times larger than the egg of a giant squid.

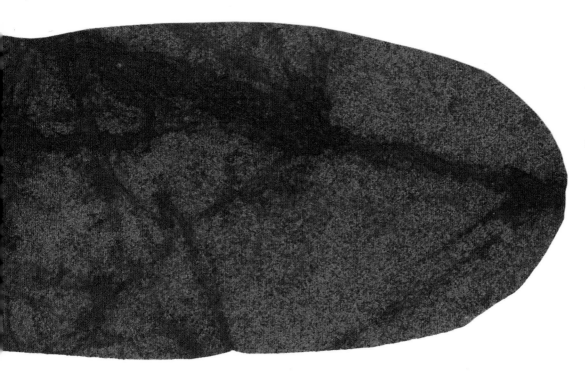

The **elephant bird, kiwi, chicken, gigantoraptor,** and **giant squid** are pictured at the same scale as an adult human.

Where should I lay my eggs?

Some animals take great pains to lay their eggs in a safe place. Others aren't so careful.

Not all animals are choosy when it's time to lay their eggs. The **horned starfish** simply releases its eggs — up to two million of them — into the water.

With her sticky saliva, the **Asian palm swift** glues two or three eggs — along with a few of her feathers — to a dangling palm frond.

The **white tern** lives on islands where there are no egg-eating animals, so she saves herself the trouble of building a nest and simply balances her egg on a bare tree branch.

A **mosquito** deposits her eggs directly on the surface of the water, where they will float until they hatch.

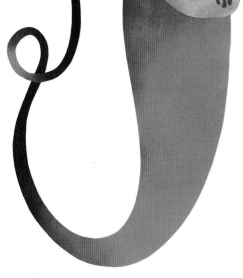

The **black-spotted sticky frog** lays her eggs in a carnivorous pitcher plant. This plant is filled with liquid that kills and digests most insects and small animals that tumble in, but the eggs and tadpoles of the sticky frog are immune to its effects.

The **Julia butterfly** perches her egg on the curling tendril of a plant, where it is less likely to be eaten by other insects.

 When it's time for the **common green lacewing** to lay her eggs, she produces dozens of long thin stalks and attaches them to a leaf. Then she places an egg at the end of each stalk, putting it out of reach of hungry ants.

More places to lay eggs . . .

The **spider wasp** stings a spider, paralyzing but not killing it. The wasp lays a single egg on the spider's abdomen, then seals its victim into a burrow. The unlucky spider will be food for the wasp larva when it emerges.

A mother **splash tetra** leaps from the water and attaches her eggs to an overhanging leaf. The father remains nearby and frequently splashes the eggs to keep them moist. As soon as they hatch, the baby fish drop into the water.

The **common murre** lays its eggs on a rocky seaside ledge. A round egg might tumble off, but the conical shape of the murre egg causes it to roll in a circle.

The female **acorn weevil** drills into an acorn with her long snout and places her eggs inside. When they hatch, the larvae will have a nutritious food source.

A **cowbird** sneaks her egg into a bluebird's nest. When it hatches, the bluebird parents will raise the cowbird chick as one of their own.

Ocean tides are highest twice a month during a full moon or new moon. It is then that thousands of **grunion** wriggle onto the beach and bury their eggs in the sand. In about two weeks another extreme tide signals the eggs to hatch and washes the baby fish out to sea.

How many eggs?

Animals that lay just a few eggs have a lot invested in each one, so they usually take good care of them. Other creatures employ a different strategy. They produce vast quantities of eggs, then pay little attention to them. Most will not survive, but there is a good chance that at least a few will hatch.

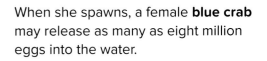

The **royal albatross** lays one egg every two years. The mother and father will take turns sitting on their egg for the next 70 or 80 days.

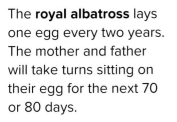

When she spawns, a female **blue crab** may release as many as eight million eggs into the water.

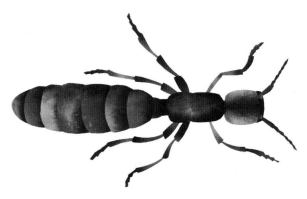

A **driver ant** colony stays on the move, devouring any animal that doesn't get out of its way. But the colony stops for a few days every month, allowing the queen to lay three or four million eggs. Then it moves on.

A female **Noble's pygmy frog** lays two eggs at a time. She will guard them and keep them moist until they hatch.

The **fish tapeworm** is a parasite that lives in the intestines of fish and animals that eat fish, including humans. A tapeworm can produce a million eggs a day for 20 years — more than seven billion eggs in its lifetime.

A **green sea turtle** often swims thousands of miles to lay her eggs, returning to the same beach where she was born. She buries 100 to 200 eggs in the sand, then returns to the sea.

Egg eaters

An egg contains all the nutrition needed by the animal growing inside. It is a concentrated source of food and an important part of many predatory animals' diets. Some of these animals have creative ways of getting to the food inside an egg.

An ostrich egg is a prize for any egg eater, but its tough shell is not easy to crack. The **Egyptian vulture** uses a tool — a rock it picks up in its beak — to break the egg open.

The predatory **spectral bat** preys on birds and mammals — including other bats. It also eats eggs, and it will quickly devour these tiny hummingbird eggs.

The **kampango**, an African catfish, lays two kinds of eggs. One kind will hatch, producing a new generation of fish. Others are unfertilized and will not hatch. The mother lays them to serve as food for the baby catfish.

Eggs are one of the favorite foods of the **mongoose**. When an egg is too tough to bite into, the mongoose has been known to hurl it backwards between its legs and smash it on a rock.

The **egg-eating snake** can swallow an egg much larger than its head. The snake pierces the egg with sharp bones at the back of its throat, squeezes out the contents, then spits out the shell.

With its long bill, the **toucan** reaches into the nests of other birds and steals their eggs.

Egg protection

Many animals ignore their eggs as soon as they are laid. But some creatures have clever ways of keeping their eggs safe. They stand guard, camouflage their eggs, or rely on poison or trickery to give their future offspring the best chance of survival.

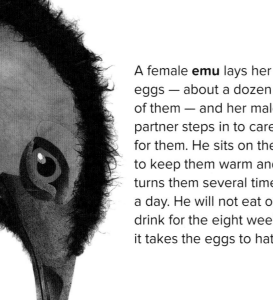

A female **emu** lays her eggs — about a dozen of them — and her male partner steps in to care for them. He sits on them to keep them warm and turns them several times a day. He will not eat or drink for the eight weeks it takes the eggs to hatch.

A mother **cuttlefish** places each of her eggs in its own capsule, then injects the capsule with black ink that will help keep the eggs hidden.

The aquatic **apple snail** lives in ponds and streams, but lays its eggs above the water. Their bright pink color warns predators that these eggs are poisonous.

To an ant, the cap on the end of the **Goliath walking stick insect** egg smells like a tasty plant seed. The egg is dropped on the ground where ants will find it and carry it into their nest. They eat the cap, but the egg is unharmed. When it hatches, the walking stick leaves the nest without being attacked.

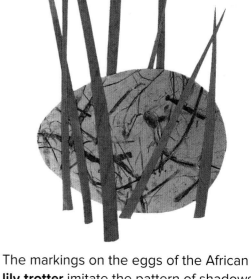

The female **hibiscus harlequin bug** defends her eggs. If danger threatens, she releases a stinky, bad-tasting liquid.

A female **five-lined skink** watches over her eggs for several months. After the baby lizards emerge from their shells, the mother eats any of the eggs that did not hatch.

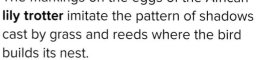

The markings on the eggs of the African **lily trotter** imitate the pattern of shadows cast by grass and reeds where the bird builds its nest.

Egg packaging

All eggs are protected by some sort of shell or membrane. Many animals go further, fabricating cases, additional shells, or other structures that keep their eggs from scattering, drifting away, or being eaten by predators.

 The **American toad** lays its eggs in ponds and streams. The eggs are contained in strips of jelly, which snag on water plants and keep the eggs from getting washed away.

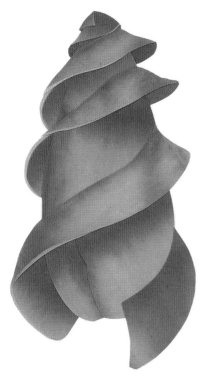

The egg case of the **horn shark** looks like a giant screw. The mother shark wedges her egg into a crevice in the rocks to keep it safe.

 The **moon snail** embeds thousands of eggs in a circular sand collar. The collar, which is stiff but flexible, rests on the sea floor and prevents the eggs from drifting away.

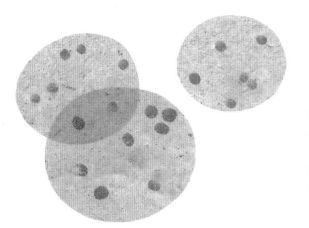

The eggs of the **volutid snail** are encased in clear, lemon-size capsules that are dispersed by ocean currents. They sometimes wash ashore in great numbers.

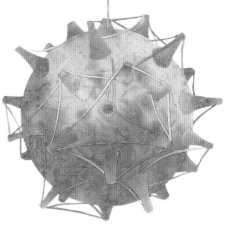

The silken egg sac of the **brown widow spider** can contain more than 200 eggs. It is suspended from a thread or entangled in the spider's web.

The **paper nautilus** is actually a kind of octopus. The female builds a delicate shell-like egg case, then moves in with the eggs until they hatch.

Carrying eggs

Some animals keep their eggs safe by taking them along wherever they go.

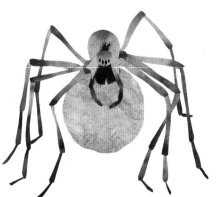

The **nursery web spider** wraps her eggs in a silk sac, which she carries in her jaws. When the eggs are almost ready to hatch, she weaves a silk tent and places the egg sac inside.

The eggs of the female **midwife toad** are encased in long strings of jelly. The male toad wraps these strings around his legs and transports the eggs until they hatch about a month later.

A female **weedy seadragon** attaches her eggs directly to the tail of her mate. He will carry them for about nine weeks until they hatch.

Workers in a **fire ant** colony constantly move the eggs laid by their queen. They take the eggs deeper into the nest at night to keep them warm or bring them closer to the surface during the day to cool them off.

The **black-eyed squid** clutches her jelly-like egg sac with sharp hooks on her tentacles. The sac contains as many as 3,000 eggs, and she will hold on to it for months, going without food until the eggs hatch.

The female **marsupial frog** has a pouch on her back that harbors her eggs until they hatch. Her male partner helps her put her eggs into the pouch as soon as she lays them.

The male **jawfish** is a mouthbrooder — it protects its mate's eggs by holding them in its mouth. It won't be able to eat for the five to seven days it takes the eggs to hatch.

Incubation

Many animals play an active role in the development of their eggs by incubating them — keeping them at the right temperature until they hatch.

A mother **platypus** keeps her one or two eggs warm by clutching them between her body and her tail.

These are the fossilized eggs of a **protoceratops**, a dinosaur the size of a black bear that lived about 75 million years ago. The fossils, which show the eggs carefully arranged in a nest, tell us that these dinosaurs probably guarded and incubated their eggs.

The **maleo** doesn't sit on her nest. Instead, she buries her eggs in beach sand heated by the sun, or in the warm ashes near an active volcano.

Snakes are cold-blooded. But by coiling around her eggs and shivering, a mother **python** can warm them up.

A mother **emperor penguin** lays an egg, then helps the father roll it onto his feet. He keeps it warm in his brood pouch — a flap of feathered skin. The father will incubate the egg for two months, going without food the entire time.

A female **alligator** buries her eggs in a large mound of leaves and sticks, where heat produced by the decomposing plants incubates the eggs. The sex of a baby alligator is determined by temperature. Warmer parts of the nest produce males, cooler ones, females.

Getting out of the egg

Eggs work beautifully to protect and nurture an unborn animal. Sooner or later, however, every animal has to get out of its egg. Eggs can be tough and strong, so this isn't always easy. It's also important that eggs hatch at the right time. A baby that emerges from its egg long after its brothers and sisters have hatched may find itself alone, without protection — easy prey for predators. Many creatures have evolved techniques for getting out of an egg or figuring out the best time to hatch.

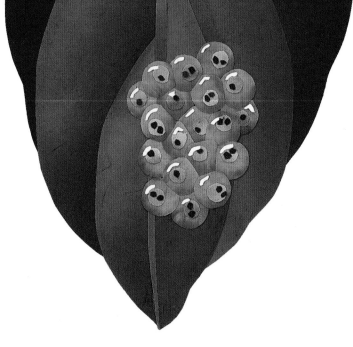

Red-eyed tree frog eggs usually take six or eight days to hatch. But if they are at least four days old, the eggs will hatch immediately if they are disturbed by a snake or other predator, and the tadpoles will drop into the water.

While still inside their eggs, baby **alligators** cheep to let their mother know they are ready to hatch, and she digs the eggs out of the nest. If the babies can't get out on their own, she will gently roll the eggs in her mouth, helping to crack them open.

The **corn snake** has a special egg tooth on its snout, which helps the snake cut its way out of its egg. The tooth will drop off a few days after the snake hatches.

The eggs of the **brine shrimp** can remain dormant, not hatching for as long as fifty years. Then, when the temperature and salt content of the water is just right, the eggs can hatch within hours.

When it's ready to hatch, a **gray partridge** chick makes a clicking sound in its shell. This tells its brothers and sisters that it's time to emerge. The eggs may have been laid days apart, but the chicks will all hatch within a few hours of each other.

The **kiwi** egg has a tough shell. The chick uses its beak to crack the eggshell, then kicks its way out with its big feet.

Inside the egg

In many ways, the animal egg is a perfect package, one that provides nutrition, shelter, and protection. We've seen how eggs vary in size and shape, how they are laid, protected, incubated, and sometimes eaten. But what goes on inside an egg? Turn the page to find out.

Inside a chicken egg

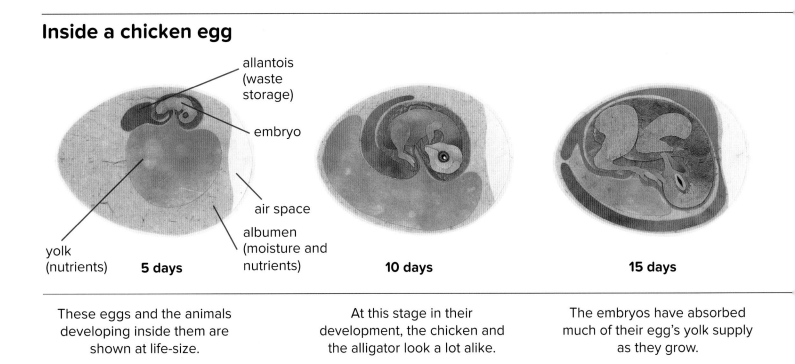

allantois (waste storage)

embryo

air space

albumen (moisture and nutrients)

yolk (nutrients)

5 days

10 days

15 days

These eggs and the animals developing inside them are shown at life-size.

At this stage in their development, the chicken and the alligator look a lot alike.

The embryos have absorbed much of their egg's yolk supply as they grow.

Inside an alligator egg

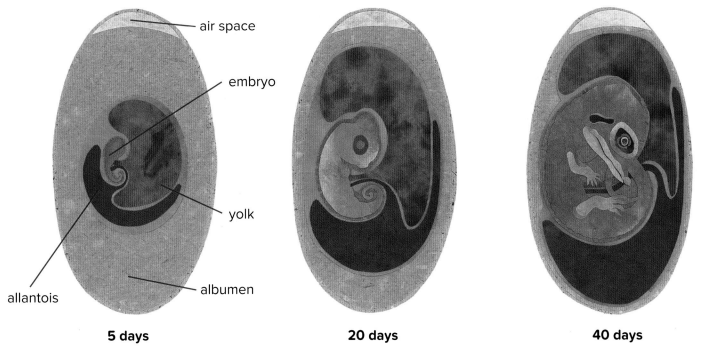

air space

embryo

yolk

allantois

albumen

5 days

20 days

40 days

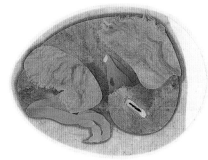

20 days

21 days

Both the chicken and alligator
have developed an egg tooth
that will help them hatch.

Time to leave the egg!

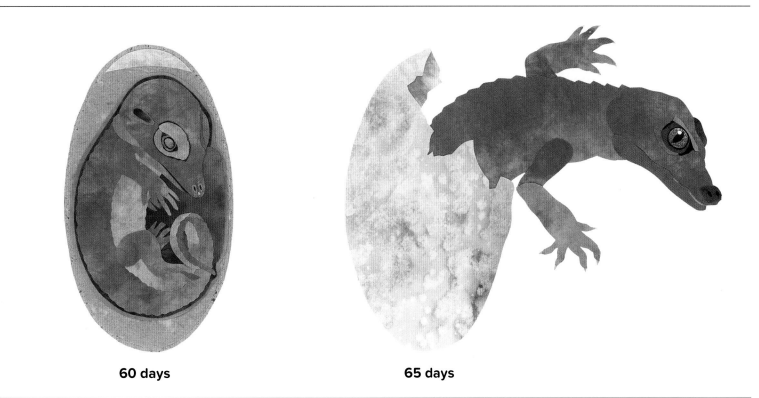

60 days

65 days

Here is more information about many of the animals in this book.

acorn weevil
length: ¼ inch (6 millimeters)
habitat: central and southern Europe
diet: acorns and hickory nuts

alligator
length: 13 feet (4 meters)
habitat: freshwater lakes, ponds, rivers, and marshes in the southeast U.S.
diet: fish, turtles, birds, deer, and other mammals, including (rarely) humans

American toad
length: 3 inches (7½ centimeters)
habitat: eastern U.S. and Canada
diet: insects, spiders, and worms

apple snail
length: up to 6 inches (15 centimeters)
habitat: tropical and subtropical freshwater lakes, ponds, and streams worldwide
diet: water plants and algae

Asian palm swift
length: 5 inches (13 centimeters)
habitat: tropical Asia
diet: insects

black-eyed squid
length: 13 inches (33 centimeters)
habitat: northern Pacific Ocean
diet: fish and crustaceans

black-spotted sticky frog
length: 2 inches (5 centimeters)
habitat: rainforests of south China and Southeast Asia
diet: insects and other invertebrates

blue crab
width: 9 inches (23 centimeters)
habitat: shallow ocean waters of the western Atlantic and the Gulf of Mexico
diet: mollusks, worms, small fish, and plants

brine shrimp
length: ⅜ inch (10 millimeters)
habitat: inland saltwater lakes worldwide
diet: algae

brown widow spider
diameter: 1½ inches (38 millimeters)
habitat: near buildings in most tropical and semitropical parts of the world
diet: insects

common green lacewing
length: ¾ inch (19 millimeters)
habitat: throughout temperate North America
diet: aphids, mites, and beetle larvae

common murre
wingspan: 26 inches (66 centimeters)
habitat: Atlantic and Pacific coasts of the U.S. and Canada
diet: small fish, squid, and crustaceans

corn snake
length: up to 6 feet (183 centimeters)
habitat: southeastern U.S.
diet: small mammals, birds, bird eggs, reptiles, and amphibians

cowbird
wingspan: 14 inches (36 centimeters)
habitat: fields and meadows of North America
diet: grass, seeds, and insects

cuttlefish
length: 10 inches (25 centimeters)
habitat: warm ocean waters worldwide
diet: fish, shrimp, and crabs

driver ant
length: (worker) ⅕ inch (5 millimeters)
habitat: rainforests and savannas in West Africa and the Congo
diet: any animal that doesn't get out of the way

egg-eating snake
length: 30 inches (76 centimeters)
habitat: Africa, India
diet: bird eggs

Egyptian vulture
wingspan: 65 inches (165 centimeters)
habitat: dry regions of southern Europe, western Asia, and northern and central Africa
diet: carrion (dead animals), eggs, small mammals, birds, and reptiles

emu
height: up to 6 feet (183 centimeters)
habitat: throughout Australia
diet: seeds, leaves, grasses, and insects

fire ant
length: (worker) ¼ inch (6 millimeters)
habitat: open areas in most tropical and subtropical parts of the world
diet: plants, seeds, insects

fish tapeworm
length: up to 33 feet (10 meters)
habitat: temperate freshwater lakes, ponds, and streams worldwide; the intestines of its host animal
diet: nutrients from its host's intestines

five-lined skink
length: 8 inches (20 centimeters)
habitat: wooded parts of the eastern U.S. and southeastern Canada
diet: insects, spiders, and worms

Goliath walking stick insect
length: 10 inches (25 centimeters)
habitat: throughout much of Australia
diet: leaves

gray partridge
length: 12 inches (30 centimeters)
habitat: farmland and open woodlands of Europe, western Asia, and central North America
diet: leaves, seeds, and insects

green sea turtle
length: 5 feet (1½ meters)
habitat: tropical and subtropical ocean waters worldwide
diet: juveniles eat jellyfish; adults eat sea grass and algae

grunion
length: 6 inches (15 centimeters)
habitat: Pacific coasts of the U.S. and Mexico
diet: plankton

hibiscus harlequin bug
length: ¾ inch (19 millimeters)
habitat: forests of northern and eastern Australia; New Guinea
diet: plant sap

horn shark
length: 4 feet (122 centimeters)
habitat: subtropical shallow waters
diet: shrimp, crabs, small fish, and other small animals

horned starfish
size: 12 inches (30 centimeters)
habitat: shallow Indo-Pacific Ocean waters
diet: mollusks, worms, and sponges

jawfish
length: 5 inches (13 centimeters)
habitat: coral reefs in the Atlantic, Pacific, and Indian Oceans and the Gulf of Mexico
diet: shrimp, worms, and other small marine animals

Julia butterfly
wingspan: 3½ inches (89 millimeters)
habitat: meadows and grasslands from Brazil through the southeast U.S.
diet: flower nectar

kampango
length: 18 inches (46 centimeters)
habitat: Lake Malawi in East Africa
diet: small fish

kiwi
length: 16 inches (41 centimeters)
habitat: temperate forests of New Zealand
diet: insects, worms, and small amphibians

lily trotter
length: 15 inches (38 centimeters)
habitat: wetlands of Central and South America, Africa, Australia, and Southeast Asia
diet: fish, insects, snails, and water plants

maleo
length: 22 inches (56 centimeters)
habitat: two volcanic islands in Indonesia
diet: fruit, seeds, and insects

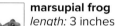
marsupial frog
length: 3 inches (7½ centimeters)
habitat: forests of Central and South America
diet: insects and worms

midwife toad
length: 2 inches (5 centimeters)
habitat: fields and forests of western Europe, near water
diet: insects and worms

mongoose
length: 2 feet (61 centimeters)
habitat: much of Africa, the Middle East, and southern Asia
diet: insects, frogs, snakes, birds, rodents, eggs, and plants

moon snail
diameter: 5½ inches (14 centimeters)
habitat: sandy sea floors worldwide
diet: shellfish, including other moon snails

mosquito
length: ⅜ inch (10 millimeters)
habitat: worldwide except Antarctica
diet: animal blood

Noble's pygmy frog
size: ½ inch (12 millimeters)
habitat: the Peruvian Andes
diet: unknown (this frog was discovered in 2009)

nursery web spider
diameter: 3 inches (7½ centimeters)
habitat: worldwide except for arctic and some desert regions
diet: insects, worms, and small fish

paper nautilus
length: up to 12 inches (30 centimeters)
habitat: tropical and subtropical ocean waters worldwide
diet: crustaceans, mollusks, and jellyfish

platypus
length: 20 inches (51 centimeters)
habitat: lakes and streams in Australia and Tasmania
diet: crayfish, insect larva, and worms

protoceratops
length: 6 feet (183 centimeters)
habitat: plains of what is now central Asia (about 75 million years ago)
diet: plants

red-eyed tree frog
length: 2 inches (5 centimeters)
habitat: rainforests of Central America
diet: insects

royal albatross
wingspan: 11 feet (3½ meters)
habitat: coastlines and islands of the southern Pacific Ocean
diet: fish, squid, and crustaceans

spectral bat
wingspan: 30 inches (76 centimeters)
habitat: forests of Central America and northern South America
diet: birds, eggs, small mammals, reptiles, and amphibians

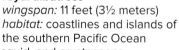

spider wasp
size: 1 inch (2½ centimeters)
habitat: worldwide except arctic regions
diet: larvae eat spiders, adults are plant-eaters

splash tetra
length: 3 inches (7½ centimeters)
habitat: tropical South American rivers
diet: insects

toucan
length: 20 inches (51 centimeters)
habitat: jungles of Central America and northern South America
diet: fruit, insects, lizards, and eggs

volutid snail
shell length: 15 inches (38 centimeters)
habitat: shallow sea floors along the Atlantic coast of South America
diet: other shellfish

weedy seadragon
length: up to 18 inches (46 centimeters)
habitat: coastal ocean waters of southern Australia
diet: animal plankton

white tern
wingspan: 30 inches (76 centimeters)
habitat: coral islands in the tropical Indian, Pacific, and Atlantic Oceans
diet: fish, crustaceans, and squid

Additional Reading

Animals and Their Eggs. By Renne. Garth Stevens Publishing, 2000.

Animal Eggs. By Dawn Cusik and Joanne O'Sullivan. Earlylight Books, 2011.

Eggs. By Marilyn Singer. Holiday House, 2008.

Eggs and Creatures That Hatch from Them. By Melvin John Uhl. Melmont Publishers, 1966.

How Animals Live. By Bernard Stonehouse and Esther Bertram. Scholastic Reference, 2004.

How Animals Work. By David Burnie. Dorling Kindersley, 2010.

The Encyclopedia of Animals. Edited by Dr. Harold G. Cogger, Joseph Forshaw, and Dr. Edward G. Zweifel. Fog City Press, 1993.

The Nature and Science of Eggs. By Jane Burton and Kim Taylor. Garth Stevens Publishing, 1998.

The Private Lives of Animals. By Roger Caras. Grosset & Dunlap, 1974.

The Way Nature Works. Edited by Robin Rees. Macmillan, 1992.

Whose Egg Is This? By Lisa J. Amstutz. Capstone Press, 2012.

For Margaret Raymo — S.J & R.P.

Text copyright © 2015 by Robin Page and Steve Jenkins

Illustrations copyright © 2015 by Steve Jenkins

www.hmhco.com

The text of this book is set in Proxmia Nova.

The illustrations are torn- and cut-paper collage.

Library of Congress Cataloging-in-Publication Data is on file.

ISBN 978-0-547-95909-2

Manufactured in China

SCP 10 9 8 7 6 5 4 3 2 1

4500505654